Adventurers

Splash in a **Pond**

by Dana Meachen Rau

Photographs by Romie Flanagan

THE ROURKE PRESS
Vero Beach, Florida

For Charlie.

—D. M. R.

Thanks to the Patel family and the North Park Nature Center for providing the modeling and location for this book.

Photographs ©: Flanagan Publishing Services/Romie Flanagan

An Editorial Directions Book

Book design and production by Ox and Company

Library of Congress Cataloging-in-Publication Data

Rau, Dana Meachen, 1971–
    Splash in a pond / Dana Meachen Rau.
        p. cm. — (The adventurers)
    Includes index.
    Summary : Illustrations and brief text describe a visit to a pond, including clothes, equipment, and things to see and do.
ISBN 1-57103-319-X
[1. Ponds—Fiction.] I. Title.
PZ7.R193975 Sp 2000
[E]—dc21

                                                    99-086594

© 2001 The Rourke Press, Inc.

Printed in the United States of America.

Are you ready for an adventure?

There are many things to see and do when you splash in a pond!

Tall boots.

Bug spray.

Magnifying glass.

That's what I *wear* when
I splash in a pond.

Diving geese.

Swimming frogs.

Floating lilies.

That's what I *see* when
I splash in a pond.

Cross a bridge.

Search for tadpoles.

Look through mud.

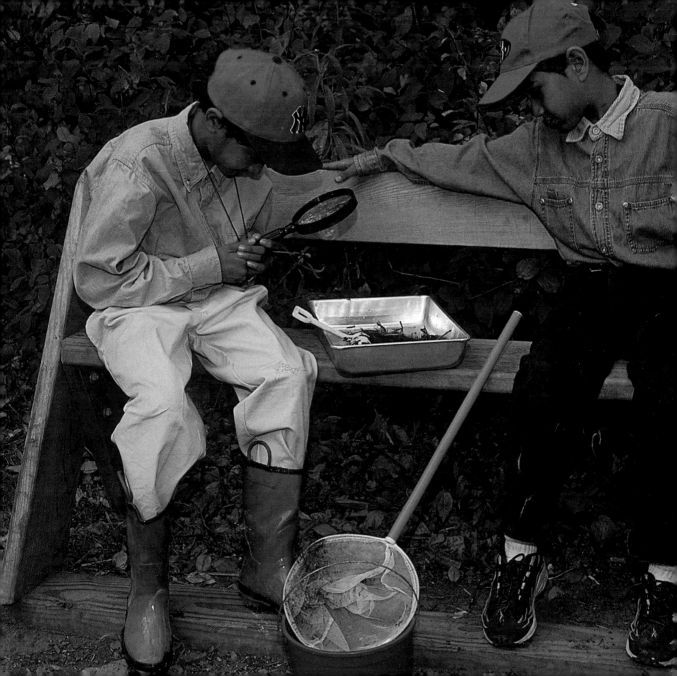

That's what I *do* when
I splash in a pond.

More Information about Ponds

A pond is a body of water that stands still. Some animals only come there for a drink. Others live in and around the pond. You can find beavers, frogs, ducks, turtles, mosquitoes, and many other animals in a pond. Even plants grow up from the bottom of the pond and float on the surface of the water.

To Find Out More about Your Environment

Books

Chinery, Michael. *Questions and Answers about Freshwater Animals.* New York: Kingfisher Books, 1994.

Fowler, Allan. *Life in a Pond.* Danbury, Conn.: Children's Press, 1996.

Stille, Darlene R. *Wetlands.* Danbury, Conn.: Children's Press, 1999.

Taylor, Barbara. *Pond Life.* New York: Dorling Kindersley, Inc., 1992.

Web Sites

The Evergreen Project Adventures
http://mbgnet.mobot.org
This site is devoted to teaching kids about environments.

U.S. Fish and Wildlife Service
http://www.fws.gov
This site is dedicated to preserving the environment and animals of America.

About the Author

When Dana Meachen Rau was a child, she and her mother often walked in the woods and splashed in ponds to find the creatures hiding there. Dana loved to write down her thoughts and draw pictures to remember her outdoor adventures. Today, Dana is a children's book editor and illustrator and has authored more than thirty books for children. She takes adventures with her husband, Chris, and son, Charlie, in Farmington, Connecticut.